The Man Who
Saw the Future

The Man Who Saw the Future

Edmond Hamilton

ÆGYPAN PRESS

This text, taken from the February, 1961, issue of
Amazing Stories was first published in the October,
1930, issue of *Amazing Stories.*

Special thanks to Greg Weeks, Stephen Blundell, and
the Online Distributed Proofreading Team (which can
be found at http://www.pgdp.net).

The Man Who Saw the Future
A publication of
ÆGYPAN PRESS

www.aegypan.com

*J*ean de Marselait, Inquisitor Extraordinary of the King of France, raised his head from the parchments that littered the crude desk at which he sat. His glance shifted along the long stone-walled, torchlit room to the file of mail-clad soldiers who stood like steel statues by its door. A word from him and two of them sprang forward.

"You may bring in the prisoner," he said.

The two disappeared through the door, and in moments there came a clang of opening bolts and grating of heavy hinges from somewhere in the building. Then the clang of the returning soldiers, and they entered the room with another man between them whose hands were fettered.

He was a straight figure, and was dressed in drab tunic and hose. His dark hair was long and straight, and his face held a dreaming strength, altogether different from the battered visages of the soldiers or the changeless mask of the Inquisitor. The latter regarded the prisoner for a moment, and then lifted one of the parchments from before him and read from it in a smooth, clear voice.

"Henri Lothiere, apothecary's assistant of Paris," he read, "is charged in this year of our lord one thousand four hundred and forty-four with offending against God and the king by committing the crime of sorcery."

The prisoner spoke for the first time, his voice low but steady. "I am no sorcerer, sire."

Jean de Marselait read calmly on from the parchment. "It is stated by many witnesses that for long that part of Paris, called Nanley by some, has been troubled by works of the devil.

Ever and anon great claps of thunder have been heard issuing from an open field there without visible cause. They were evidently caused by a sorcerer of power since even exorcists could not halt them.

"It is attested by many that the accused, Henri Lothiere, did in spite of the known diabolical nature of the thing, spend much time at the field in question. It is also attested that the said Henri Lothiere did state that in his opinion the thunderclaps were not of diabolical origin, and that if they were studied, their cause might be discovered.

"It being suspected from this that Henri Lothiere was himself the sorcerer causing the thunderclaps, he was watched and on the third day of June was seen to go in the early morning to the unholy spot with certain instruments. There he was observed going through strange and diabolical conjurations, when there came suddenly another thunderclap and the said Henri Lothiere did vanish entirely from view in that moment. This fact is attested beyond all doubt.

"The news spreading, many hundreds watched around the field during that day. Upon that night before midnight, another thunder-clap was heard and the said Henri Lothiere was seen by these hundreds to appear at the field's center as swiftly and as strangely as he had vanished. The fear-stricken hundreds around the field heard him tell them how, by diabolical power, he had gone for hundreds of years into the future, a thing surely possible only to the devil and his minions, and heard him tell other blasphemies before they seized him and brought him to the Inquisitor of the King, praying that he be burned and his work of sorcery thus halted.

"Therefore, Henri Lothiere, since you were seen to vanish and to reappear as only the servants of the evil one might do, and were heard by many to utter the blasphemies mentioned, I must adjudge you a sorcerer with the penalty of death by fire. If anything there be that you can advance in palliation of your black offense, however, you may now do so before final sentence is passed upon you."

Jean de Marselait laid down the parchment, and raised his eyes to the prisoner. The latter looked round him quickly for a moment, a half-glimpsed panic for an instant in his eyes, then seemed to steady.

"Sire, I cannot change the sentence you will pass upon me," he said quietly, "yet do I wish well to relate once, what happened to me and what I saw. Is it permitted me to tell that from first to last?"

The Inquisitor's head bent, and Henri Lothiere spoke, his voice gaining in strength and fervor as he continued.

"Sire, I, Henri Lothiere, am no sorcerer but a simple apothecary's assistant. It was always my nature, from earliest youth, to desire to delve into matters unknown to men; the secrets of the earth and sea and sky, the knowledge hidden from us. I knew well that this was wicked, that the Church teaches all we need to know and that heaven frowns when we pry into its mysteries, but so strong was my desire to know, that many times I concerned myself with matters forbidden.

"I had sought to know the nature of the lightning, and the manner of flight of the birds, and the way in which fishes are able to live beneath the waters, and the mystery of the stars. So when these thunderclaps began to be heard in the part of Paris in which I lived, I did not fear them so much as my neighbors. I was eager to learn only what was causing them, for it seemed to me that their cause might be learned.

"So I began to go to that field from which they issued, to study them. I waited in it and twice I heard the great thunderclaps myself. I thought they came from near the field's center, and I studied that place. But I could see nothing there that was causing them. I dug in the ground, I looked up for hours into the sky, but there was nothing. And still, at intervals, the thunderclaps sounded.

"I still kept going to the field, though I knew that many of my neighbors whispered that I was engaged in sorcery. Upon that morning of the third day of June, it had occurred to me to take certain instruments, such as loadstones, to the field, to see whether anything might be learned with them. I went, a few superstitious ones following me at a distance. I reached the field's center, and started the examinations I had planned. Then came suddenly another thunderclap and with it I passed from the sight of those who had followed and were watching, vanished from view.

"Sire, I cannot well describe what happened in that moment. I heard the thunderclap come as though from all the air around me, stunning my ears with its terrible burst of sound. And at the same moment that I heard it, I was buffeted as though by awful winds and seemed falling downward through terrific depths. Then through the hellish uproar, I felt myself bumping upon a hard surface, and the sounds quickly ceased from about me.

"I had involuntarily closed my eyes at the great thunderclap, but now, slowly, I opened them. I looked around me, first in stupefaction, and then in growing amazement. For I was not in that familiar field at all, sire, that I had been in a moment before. I was in a room, lying upon its floor, and it was such a room as I had never seen before.

"Its walls were smooth and white and gleaming. There were windows in the walls, and they were closed with sheets of glass so smooth and clear that one seemed looking through a clear opening rather than through glass. The floor was of stone, smooth and seamless as though carven from one great rock, yet seeming not, in some way, to be stone at all. There was a great circle of smooth metal inset in it, and it was on it that I was lying.

"All around the room were many great things the like of which I had never seen. Some seemed of black metal, seemed contrivances or machines of some sort. Black cords of wire connected them to each other and from part of them came a humming sound that did not stop. Others had glass tubes fixed on the front of them, and there were square black plates on which were many shining little handles and buttons.

"There was a sound of voices, and I turned to find that two men were bending over me. They were men like myself, yet they were at the same time like no men I had ever met! One was white-bearded and the other plump and bare of face. Neither of them wore cloak or tunic or hose. Instead they wore loose and straight-hanging garments of cloth.

"They were both greatly excited, it seemed, and were talking to each other as they bent over me. I caught a word or two of their speech in a moment, and found it was French they were talking. But it was not the French I knew, being so strange and with so many new words as to be almost a different language. I could understand the drift, though, of what they were saying.

"'We have succeeded!' the plump one was shouting excitedly. 'We've brought someone through at last!'

"'They will never believe it,' the other replied. 'They'll say it was faked.'

"'Nonsense!' cried the first. 'We can do it again, Rastin; we can show them before their own eyes!'

"They bent toward me, seeing me staring at them.

"'Where are you from?' shouted the plump-faced one. 'What time — what year — what century?'

"'He doesn't understand, Thicourt,' muttered the white-bearded one. 'What year is this now, my friend?' he asked me.

"I found voice to answer. 'Surely, sirs, whoever you be, you know that this is the year fourteen hundred and forty-four,' I said.

"That set them off again into a babble of excited talk, of which I could make out only a word here and there. They lifted me up, seeing how sick and weak I felt, and seated me in a strange, but very comfortable chair. I felt dazed. The two were still talking excitedly, but finally the white-bearded one, Rastin, turned to me. He spoke to me, very slowly, so that I understood him clearly, and he asked me my name. I told him.

"'Henri Lothiere,' he repeated. 'Well, Henri, you must try to understand. You are not now in the year 1444. You are five hundred years in the future, or what would seem to you the future. This is the year 1944.'

"'And Rastin and I have jerked you out of your own time across five solid centuries,' said the other, grinning.

"I looked from one to the other. 'Messieurs,' I pleaded, and Rastin shook his head.

"'He does not believe,' he said to the other. Then to me, 'Where were you just before you found yourself here, Henri?' he asked.

"'In a field at the outskirts of Paris,' I said.

"'Well, look from that window and see if you still believe yourself in your 15th-century Paris.'

"*I* went to the window. I looked out. Mother of God, what a sight before my eyes! The familiar gray little houses, the open fields behind them, the saunterers in the dirt streets — all these were gone and it was a new and terrible city that lay about me! Its broad streets were of stone and great buildings of many levels rose on either side of them. Great numbers of people, dressed like the two beside me, moved in the streets and also strange vehicles or carriages, undrawn by horse or ox, that rushed to and fro at undreamed-of speed! I staggered back to the chair.

"'You believe now, Henri?' asked the whitebeard, Rastin, kindly enough, and I nodded weakly. My brain was whirling.

"He pointed to the circle of metal on the floor and the machines around the room. 'Those are what we used to jerk you from your own time to this one,' he said.

"'But how, sirs?' I asked. 'For the love of God, how is it that you can take me from one time to another? Have ye become gods or devils?'

"'Neither the one nor the other, Henri,' he answered. 'We are simply scientists, physicists — men who want to know as much as man can know and who spend our lives in seeking knowledge.'

"I felt my confidence returning. These were men such as I had dreamed might some day be. 'But what can you do with time?' I asked. 'Is not time a thing unalterable, unchanging?'

"Both shook their heads. 'No, Henri, it is not. But lately have our men of science found that out.'

"They went on to tell me of things that I could not understand. It seemed they were telling that their men of knowledge had found time to be a mere measurement, or dimension, just as length or breadth or thickness. They mentioned names with reverence that I had never heard — Einstein and De Sitter and Lorentz. I was in a maze at their words.

"They said that just as men use force to move or rotate matter from one point along the three known measurements to another, so might matter be rotated from one point in time, the fourth measurement, to another, if the right force were used. They said that their machines produced that force and applied it to the metal circle from five hundred years before to this time of theirs.

"They had tried it many times, they said, but nothing had been on the spot at that time and they had rotated nothing but the air above it from the one time to the other, and the reverse. I told them of the thunderclaps that had been heard at the spot in the field and that had made me curious. They said that they had been caused by the changing of the air above the spot from the one time to the other in their trials. I could not understand these things.

"They said then that I had happened to be on the spot when they had again turned on their force and so had been rotated out of my own time into theirs. They said that they had always hoped to get someone living from a distant time in that way, since such a man would be a proof to all the other men of knowledge of what they had been able to do.

"I could not comprehend, and they saw and told me not to fear. I was not fearful, but excited at the things that I saw around me. I asked of those things and Rastin and Thicourt laughed and explained some of them to me as best they could. Much they said that I did not understand but my eyes saw marvels in that room of which I had never dreamed.

"They showed me a thing like a small glass bottle with wires inside, and then told me to touch a button beneath it. I did so and the bottle shone with a brilliant light exceeding that of scores of candles. I shrank back, but they laughed, and when Rastin touched the button again, the light in the glass thing vanished. I saw that there were many of these things in the ceiling.

"They showed me also a rounded black object of metal with a wheel at the end. A belt ran around the wheel and around smaller wheels connected to many machines. They touched a lever on this object and a sound of humming came from it and the wheel turned very fast, turning all the machines with the belt. It turned faster than any man could ever have turned it, yet when they touched the lever again, its turning ceased. They said that it was the power of the lightning in the skies that they used to make the light and to turn that wheel!

"My brain reeled at the wonders that they showed. One took an instrument from the table that he held to his face, saying that he would summon the other scientists or men of knowledge to see their experiment that night. He spoke into the instrument as though to different men, and let me hear voices from it answering him! They said that the men who answered were leagues separated from him!

"I could not believe — and yet somehow I did believe! I was half-dazed with wonder and yet excited too. The white-bearded man, Rastin, saw that, and encouraged me. Then they brought a small box with an opening and placed a black disk on the box, and set it turning in some way. A woman's voice came from the opening of the box, singing. I shuddered when they told me that the woman was one who had died years before. Could the dead speak thus?

"*H*ow can I describe what I saw there? Another box or cabinet there was, with an opening also. I thought it was like that from which I had heard the dead woman singing, but they said it was different. They touched buttons on it and a voice came from it speaking in a tongue I knew not. They said that the man was speaking thousands of leagues from us, in a strange land across the uncrossed western ocean, yet he seemed speaking by my side!

"They saw how dazed I was by these things, and gave me wine. At that I took heart, for wine, at least, was as it had always been.

"'You will want to see Paris — the Paris of our time, Henri?' asked Rastin.

"'But it is different — terrible —' I said.

"'We'll take you,' Thicourt said, 'but first your clothes —'

"He got a long light coat that they had me put on, that covered my tunic and hose, and a hat of grotesque round shape that they put on my head. They led me then out of the building and into the street.

"I gazed astoundedly along that street. It had a raised walk at either side, on which many hundreds of people moved to and fro, all dressed in as strange a fashion. Many, like Rastin and Thicourt, seemed of gentle blood, yet, in spite of this, they did not wear a sword or even a dagger. There were no knights or squires, or priests or peasants. All seemed dressed much the same.

"Small lads ran to and fro selling what seemed sheets of very thin white parchment, many times folded and covered with lettering. Rastin said that these had written in them all things that had happened through all the world, even but hours before. I said that to write even one of these sheets would take a clerk many days, but they said that the writing was done in some way very quickly by machines.

"In the broad stone street between the two raised walks were rushing back and forth the strange vehicles I had seen from the window. There was no animal pulling or pushing any one of them, yet they never halted their swift rush, and carried many people at unthinkable speed. Sometimes those who walked stepped before the rushing vehicles, and then from them came terrible warning snarls or moans that made the walkers draw back.

"One of the vehicles stood at the walk's edge before us, and we entered it and sat side by side on a soft leather seat. Thicourt sat behind a wheel on a post, with levers beside him. He touched these and a humming sound came from somewhere in the vehicle and then it too began to rush forward. Faster and faster along the street it went, yet neither of them seemed afraid.

"Many thousands of these vehicles were moving swiftly through the streets about us. We passed on, between great buildings and along wider streets, my eyes and ears numbed by what I saw about me. Then the buildings grew smaller, after we had gone for miles through them, and we were passing through the city's outskirts. I could not believe, hardly, that it was Paris in which I was.

"We came to a great flat and open field outside the city and there Thicourt stopped and we got out of the vehicle. There were big buildings at the field's end, and I saw other vehicles rolling out of them across the field, ones different from any I had yet seen, with flat winglike projections on either side. They rolled out over the field very fast and then I cried out as I saw them rising from the ground into the air. Mother of God, they were flying! The men in them were flying!

"Rastin and Thicourt took me forward to the great buildings. They spoke to men there and one brought forward one of the winged cars. Rastin told me to get in, and though I was terribly afraid, there was too terrible a fascination that drew me in. Thicourt and Rastin entered after me, and we sat in seats with the other man. He had before him levers and buttons, while at the car's front was a great thing like a double-oar or paddle. A loud roaring came and that double-blade began to whirl so swiftly that I could not see it. Then the car rolled swiftly forward, bumping on the ground, and then ceased to bump. I looked down, then shuddered. The ground was already far beneath! I too, was flying in the air!

"We swept upward at terrible speed that increased steadily. The thunder of the car was terrific, and, as the man at the levers changed their position, we curved around and over downward and upward as though birds. Rastin tried to explain to me how the car flew, but it was all too wonderful, and I could not understand. I only knew that a wild thrilling excitement held me, and that it were worth life and death to fly thus, if but for once, as I had always dreamed that men might some day do.

"Higher and higher we went. The earth lay far beneath and I saw now that Paris was indeed a mighty city, its vast mass of buildings stretching away almost to the horizons below us. A mighty city of the future that it had been given my eyes to look on!

"There were other winged cars darting to and fro in the air about us, and they said that many of these were starting or finishing journeys of hundreds of leagues in the air. Then I cried out as I saw a great shape coming nearer us in the air. It was many rods in length, tapering to a point at both ends, a vast ship sailing in the air! There were great cabins on its lower part and in them we glimpsed people gazing out, coming and going inside, dancing even! They told me that vast ships of the air like this sailed to and fro for thousands of leagues with hundreds inside them.

"The huge vessel of the air passed us and then our winged car began to descend. It circled smoothly down to the field like a swooping bird, and, when we landed there, Rastin and Thicourt led me back to the ground-vehicle. It was late afternoon by then, the sun sinking westward, and darkness had descended by the time we rolled back into the great city.

"But in that city was not darkness! Lights were everywhere in it, flashing brilliant lights that shone from its mighty buildings and that blinked and burned and ran like water in great symbols upon the buildings above the streets. Their glare was like that of day! We stopped before a great building into which Rastin and Thicourt led me.

"It was vast inside and in it were many people in rows on rows of seats. I thought it a cathedral at first but saw soon that it was not. The wall at one end of it, toward which all in it were gazing, had on it pictures of people, great in size, and those pictures were moving as though themselves alive! And they were talking one to another, too, as though with living voices! I trembled. What magic!

"With Rastin and Thicourt in seats beside me, I watched the pictures enthralled. It was like looking through a great window into strange worlds. I saw the sea, seemingly tossing and roaring there before me, and then saw on it a ship, a vast ship of size incredible, without sails or oars, holding thousands of people. I seemed on that ship as I watched, seemed moving forward with it. They told me it was sailing over the western ocean that never men had crossed. I feared!

"Then another scene, land appearing from the ship. A great statue, upholding a torch, and we on the ship seemed passing beneath it. They said that the ship was approaching a city, the city of New York, but mists hid all before us. Then suddenly the mists before the ship cleared and there before me seemed the city.

"Mother of God, what a city! Climbing range on range of great mountain-like buildings that aspired up as though to scale heaven itself! Far beneath narrow streets pierced through them and in the picture we seemed to land from the ship, to go through those streets of the city. It was an incredible city of madness! The streets and ways were mere chasms between the sky-toppling buildings! People — people — people — millions on millions of them rushed through the endless streets. Countless ground-vehicles rushed to and fro also, and other different ones that roared above the streets and still others below them!

"Winged flying-cars and great airships were sailing to and fro over the titanic city, and in the waters around it great ships of the sea and smaller ships were coming as man never dreamed of surely, that reached out from the mighty city on all sides. And with the coming of darkness, the city blazed with living light!

"The pictures changed, showed other mighty cities, though none so terrible as that one. It showed great mechanisms that appalled me. Giant metal things that scooped in an instant from the earth as much as a man might dig in days. Vast things that poured molten metal from them like water. Others that lifted loads that hundreds of men and oxen could not have stirred.

"They showed men of knowledge like Rastin and Thicourt beside me. Some were healers, working miraculous cures in a way that I could not understand. Others were gazing through giant tubes at the stars, and the pictures showed what they saw, showed that all of the stars were great suns like our sun, and that our sun was greater than earth, that earth moved around it instead of the reverse! How could such things be, I wondered. Yet they said that it was so, that earth was round like an apple, and that with other earths like it, the planets, moved round the sun. I heard, but could scarce understand.

"At last Rastin and Thicourt led me out of that place of living pictures and to their ground-vehicle. We went again through the streets to their building, where first I had found myself. As we went I saw that none challenged my right to go, nor asked who was my lord. And Rastin said that none now had lords, but that all were lord, king and priest and noble, having no more power than any in the land. Each man was his own master! It was what I had hardly dared to hope for, in my own time, and this, I thought, was greatest of all the marvels they had shown me!

"We entered again their building but Rastin and Thicourt took me first to another room than the one in which I had found myself. They said that their men of knowledge were gathered there to hear of their feat, and to have it proved to them.

"'You would not be afraid to return to your own time, Henri?' asked Rastin, and I shook my head.

"'I want to return to it,' I told them. 'I want to tell my people there what I have seen — what the future is that they must strive for.'

"'But if they should not believe you?' Thicourt asked.

"'Still I must go — must tell them,' I said.

"Rastin grasped my hand. 'You are a man, Henri,' he said. Then, throwing aside the cloak and hat I had worn outside, they went with me down to the big white-walled room where first I had found myself.

"It was lit brightly now by many of the shining glass things on ceiling and walls, and in it were many men. They all stared strangely at me and at my clothes, and talked excitedly so fast that I could not understand. Rastin began to address them.

"He seemed explaining how he had brought me from my own time to his. He used many terms and words that I could not understand, incomprehensible references and phrases, and I could understand but little. I heard again the names of Einstein and De Sitter that I had heard before, repeated frequently by these men as they disputed with Rastin and Thicourt. They seemed disputing about me.

"One big man was saying, 'Impossible! I tell you, Rastin, you have faked this fellow!'

"Rastin smiled. 'You don't believe that Thicourt and I brought him here from his own time across five centuries?'

"A chorus of excited negatives answered him. He had me stand up and speak to them. They asked me many questions, part of which I could not understand. I told them of my life, and of the city of my own time, and of king and priest and noble, and of many simple things that they seemed quite ignorant of. Some appeared to believe me but others did not, and again their dispute broke out.

"'There is a way to settle the argument, gentlemen,' said Rastin finally.

"'How?' all cried.

"'Thicourt and I brought Henri across five centuries by rotating the time-dimensions at this spot,' he said. 'Suppose we reverse that rotation and send him back before your eyes — would that be proof?'

"They all said that it would. Rastin turned to me. 'Stand on the metal circle, Henri,' he said. I did so.

"All were watching very closely. Thicourt did something quickly with the levers and buttons of the mechanisms in the room. They began to hum, and blue light came from the glass tubes on some. All were quiet, watching me as I stood there on the circle of metal. I met Rastin's eyes and something in me made me call goodbye to him. He waved his hand and smiled. Thicourt pressed more buttons and the hum of the mechanisms grew louder. Then he reached toward another lever. All in the room were tense and I was tense.

"Then I saw Thicourt's arm move as he turned one of the many levers.

"A terrific clap of thunder seemed to break around me, and as I closed my eyes before its shock, I felt myself whirling around and falling at the same time as though into a maelstrom, just as I had done before. The awful falling sensation ceased in a moment and the sound subsided. I opened my eyes. I was on the ground at the center of the familiar field from which I had vanished hours before, upon the morning of that day. It was night now, though, for that day I had spent five hundred years in the future.

"There were many people gathered around the field, fearful, and they screamed and some fled when I appeared in the thunderclap. I went toward those who remained. My mind was full of things I had seen and I wanted to tell them of these things. I wanted to tell them how they must work ever toward that future time of wonder.

"But they did not listen. Before I had spoken minutes to them they cried out on me as a sorcerer and a blasphemer, and seized me and brought me here to the Inquisitor, to you, sire. And to you, sire, I have told the truth in all things. I know that in doing so I have set the seal of my own fate, and that only a sorcerer would ever tell such a tale, yet despite that I am glad. Glad that I have told one at least of this time of what I saw five centuries in the future. Glad that I saw! Glad that I saw the things that someday, sometime, must come to be —"

*I*t was a week later that they burned Henri Lothiere. Jean de Marselait, lifting his gaze from his endless parchment accusation and examens on that afternoon, looked out through the window at a thick curl of black smoke going up from the distant square.

"Strange, that one," he mused. "A sorcerer, of course, but such a one as I had never heard before. I wonder," he half-whispered, "was there any truth in that wild tale of his? The future — who can say — what men might do — ?"

There was silence in the room as he brooded for a moment, and then he shook himself as one ridding himself of absurd speculations. "But tush — enough of these crazy fancies. They will have me for a sorcerer if I yield to these wild fancies and visions *of the future.*"

And bending again with his pen to the parchment before him, he went gravely on with his work.

THE END